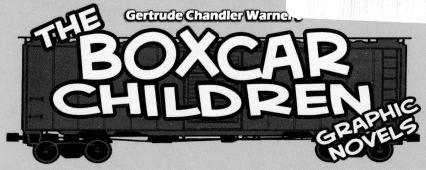

Gertrude Chandler Warner's

THE BOXCAR CHILDREN

GRAPHIC NOVELS

THE WOODSHED MYSTERY

The Alden children are staying at the New England farmhouse where their grandfather grew up. There are many legends about the old farm, especially about a woodshed near the house. Can the Boxcar Children discover the secret of the woodshed—one that goes back to the Revolutionary War?

THE BOXCAR CHILDREN
GRAPHIC NOVELS

THE BOXCAR CHILDREN
SURPRISE ISLAND
THE YELLOW HOUSE MYSTERY
MYSTERY RANCH
MIKE'S MYSTERY
BLUE BAY MYSTERY
SNOWBOUND MYSTERY
TREE HOUSE MYSTERY
THE HAUNTED CABIN MYSTERY
THE AMUSEMENT PARK MYSTERY
THE PIZZA MYSTERY
THE CASTLE MYSTERY
THE WOODSHED MYSTERY
THE LIGHTHOUSE MYSTERY
MOUNTAIN TOP MYSTERY

Gertrude Chandler Warner's

THE BOXCAR CHILDREN
THE WOODSHED MYSTERY

Adapted by Joeming Dunn
Illustrated by Ben Dunn

Henry Alden

Watch

Jessie Alden

Violet Alden

Benny Alden

Adapted by Joeming Dunn
Illustrated by Ben Dunn
Colored by Robby Bevard
Lettered by Joeming Dunn & Doug Dlin
Edited by Stephanie Hedlund
Interior layout and design by Kristen Fitzner Denton
Cover art by Ben Dunn
Book design and packaging by Shannon Eric Denton

Library of Congress Cataloging-in-Publication Data
is available from the Library of Congress.

10 9 8 7 6 5 4 3 2 1 LB 15 14 13 12 11 10

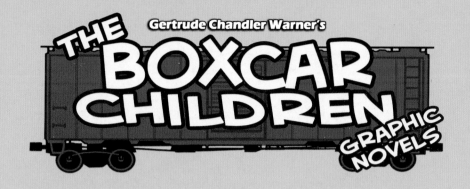

THE WOODSHED MYSTERY

Contents

A FARM FOR SALE

Hello... Oh, yes.

Just wonderful, Jane. See you soon.

One spring evening, Grandfather Alden received an exciting phone call.

Aunt Jane wants to come East to live in New England again!

She wants me to buy a farm for her right away.

Grandfather gathered Henry, Jessie, Violet, and Benny together to hear the news.

Why does she want to move? Mystery Ranch is such an exciting place to live.

Grandfather told the children that he and Jane were born on a farm here. They moved to a ranch out West when they were teenagers. Now, Jane wanted to move closer to the Aldens.

Maybe I can buy the very farm where we used to live!

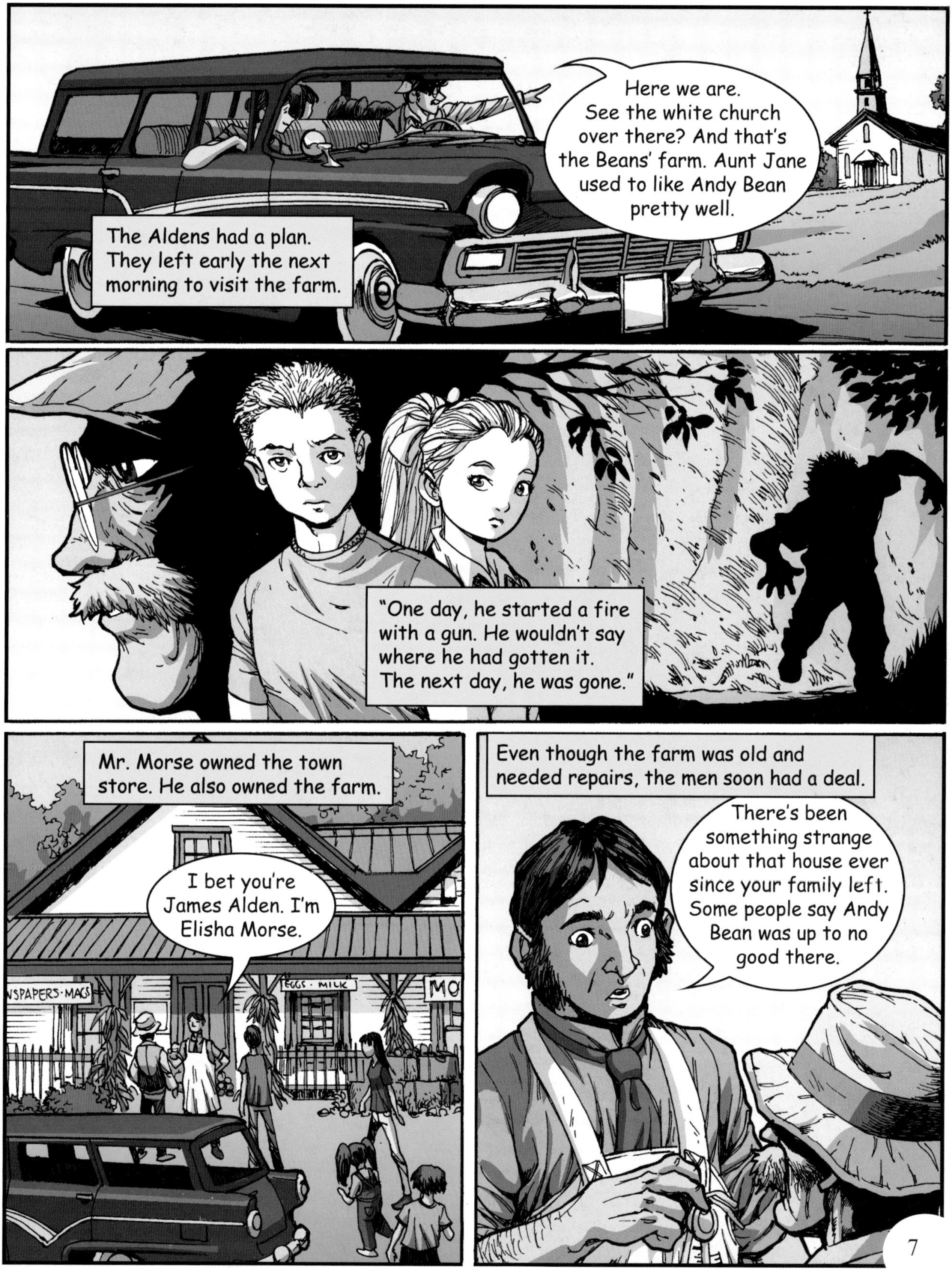
The Aldens had a plan. They left early the next morning to visit the farm.
Here we are. See the white church over there? And that's the Beans' farm. Aunt Jane used to like Andy Bean pretty well.
"One day, he started a fire with a gun. He wouldn't say where he had gotten it. The next day, he was gone."
Mr. Morse owned the town store. He also owned the farm.
I bet you're James Alden. I'm Elisha Morse.
EGGS · MILK
Even though the farm was old and needed repairs, the men soon had a deal.
There's been something strange about that house ever since your family left. Some people say Andy Bean was up to no good there.

The Aldens made their way to the farm.

Oh!

This house was built in 1750. Before the Revolutionary War!

What an enormous fireplace! Look at the old brick ovens on both sides.

GRANDFATHER TAKES OVER

Soon the house was busy with workers.

The Aldens quickly tired of watching the work. They began to explore the house.

I can't believe this cellar was here during the Revolutionary War.

I suppose people kept vegetables down here in the winter.

No potatoes here!

Grandfather says that was the potato pit.

Imagine finding a potato from Revolutionary days!

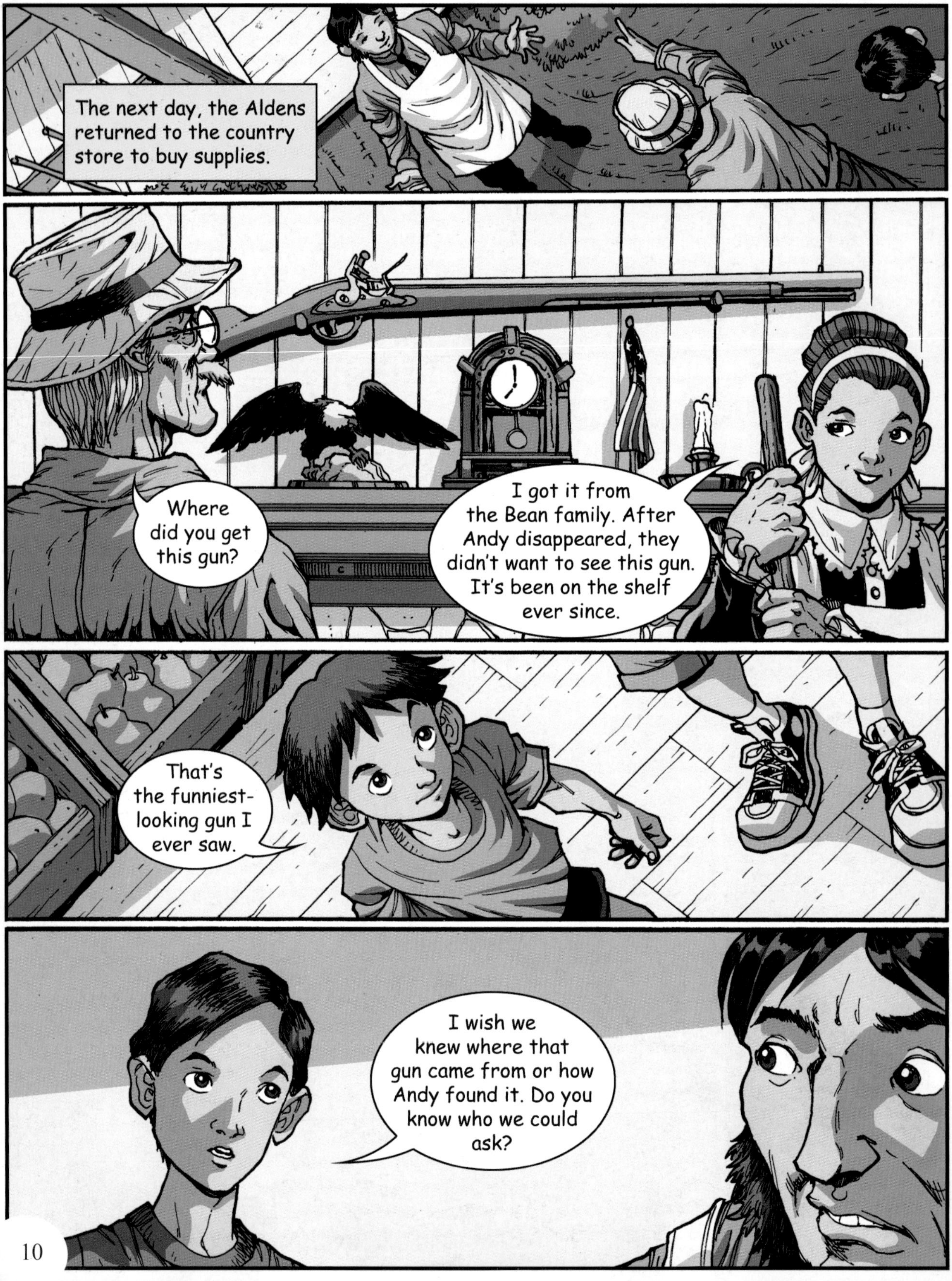
The next day, the Aldens returned to the country store to buy supplies.
Where did you get this gun?
I got it from the Bean family. After Andy disappeared, they didn't want to see this gun. It's been on the shelf ever since.
That's the funniest-looking gun I ever saw.
I wish we knew where that gun came from or how Andy found it. Do you know who we could ask?

Mr. Morse gave them directions to find the oldest man in town.

Mr. Cole was a kind gentleman who enjoyed having company.

So, what can I tell you?

I know you've heard the story of the old gun.

Yep. An old flintlock.

Where did the gun come from?

My younger brother, John Cole, might know. He lives in New York but comes up here in the summer. He'll be here in a few weeks.

Well, thank you.

EXPLORING THE WOODSHED

James, how did you ever get this farm back?

Very easily. Nobody wanted it.

Well, *I* want it. What a fine summer we'll have with the children.

Aunt Jane and the kids settled in for the summer. Everyone in town now knew the four young Aldens. Benny had just returned from visiting the Bean Farm.

Here's something funny. The Beans raise eggs.

No, Benny, they raise hens.

Anyway, they *sell* eggs. And every day about three eggs are gone.

A few weeks later, the house was done. Aunt Jane had arrived!

How do the Beans know?

They keep track of how many eggs they have. They think somebody is stealing eggs.

A mystery!

There is nothing there now except the brook and the old woodshed.

We've been everywhere in this town except the woods. Let's go in the woods today.

The kids were soon all off to see the woodshed.

It isn't much.

CREEEK

Inside, they found a surprise! Someone was staying in the woodshed!

No knife, I bet somebody has a knife right in his pocket!

There's no food either.

Yes there is. Look up!

What do you know!

An egg! This is where the eggs go!

Henry, now a bit worried, guided the kids out of the shed.

Now we have two mysteries: who takes the eggs and who lives here? Let's go.

The Aldens returned to the farm and found Grandfather. They convinced him to go see the woodshed with them.

You'll see for yourself. Go in and look around.

CLUES FROM AN OLD BOOK

...but nothing was inside!

Grandfather carefully entered the old woodshed...

They decided to tell Aunt Jane about the strange woodshed.

What a story that is!

You should find out when Grandpa Cole's brother is coming. That's what I'd do.

Mr. Cole wasn't coming for several weeks. In the meantime, Violet made an interesting discovery.

I found this book in the parlor.

John Hancock

Sam Adams

It's all about the Revolutionary War. It tells how John Hancock and Sam Adams had to hide.

Here is a picture of that old gun!

If John Hancock had to hide...

I'm sure there would be a lot of other men who had to hide, too!

What's Violet got?

She's found news about our mystery.

John Hancock's men gathered all the guns, bullets, and gunpowder they could. One time they hid guns in a load of hay. The Redcoats just stood and watched the hay go by.

Do you think any of those men hid in our woodshed?

Maybe.

Let's go back to the woodshed. This time we'll take a flashlight.

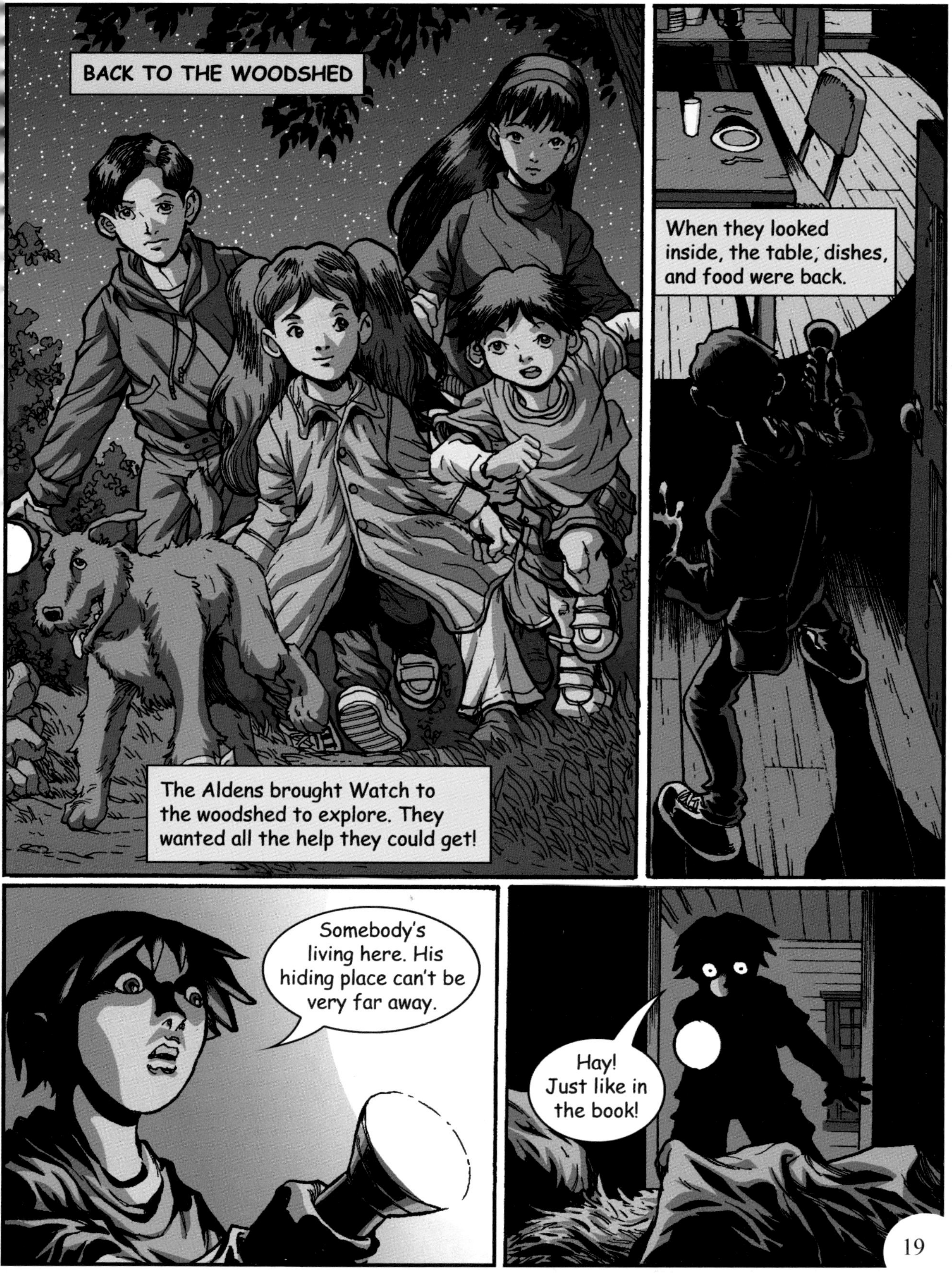
BACK TO THE WOODSHED
The Aldens brought Watch to the woodshed to explore. They wanted all the help they could get!
When they looked inside, the table, dishes, and food were back.
Somebody's living here. His hiding place can't be very far away.
Hay! Just like in the book!

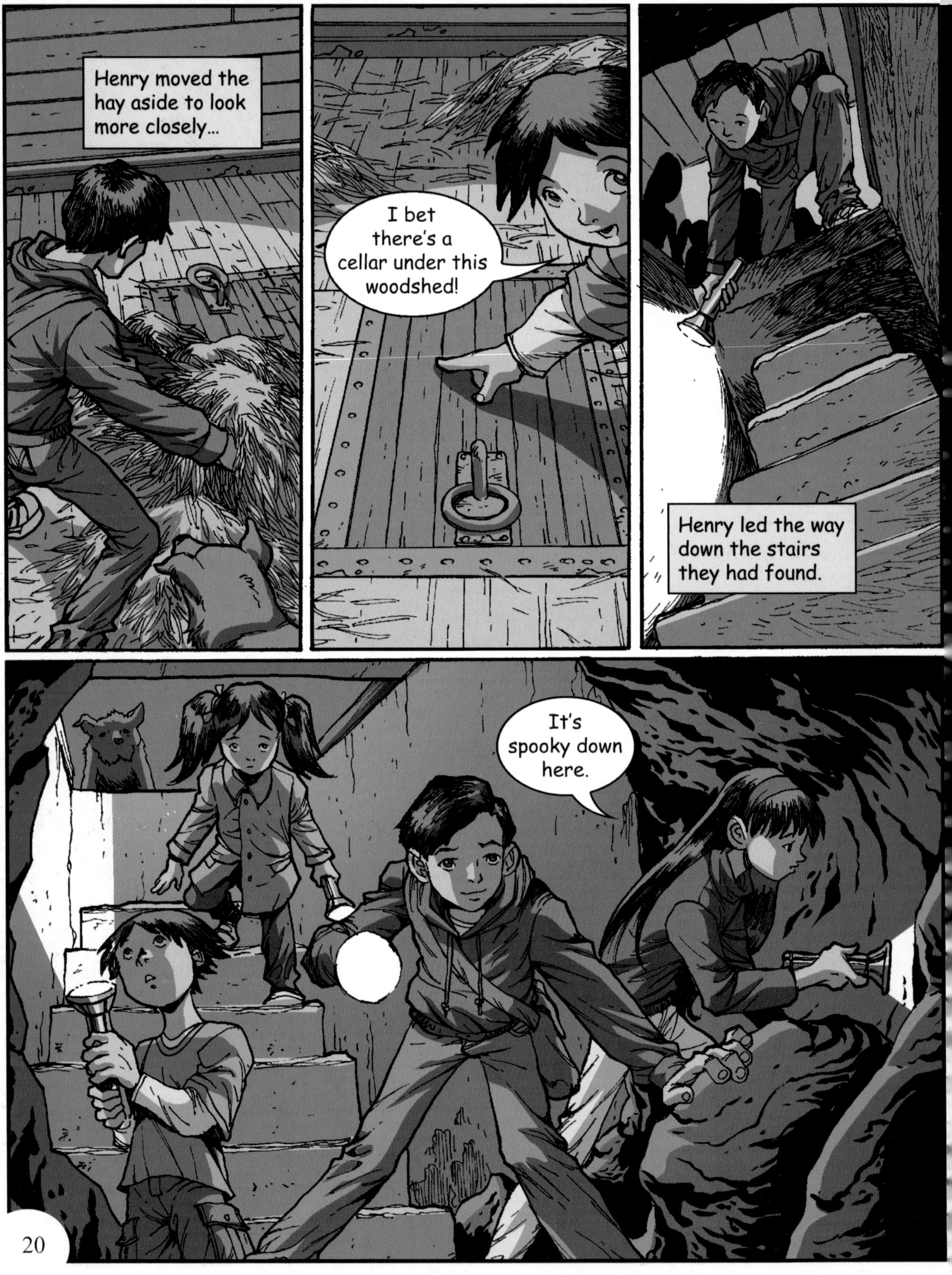
Henry moved the hay aside to look more closely...
I bet there's a cellar under this woodshed!
Henry led the way down the stairs they had found.
It's spooky down here.

OW!

Benny tripped on something hard.

That box is made of iron!

Take it, we can open it later.

Look at this! It goes farther!

We'd better tell Aunt Jane about this.

The group went to tell Aunt Jane of their discovery.

They decided to open the iron box and see what had been hidden inside.

What an old candlestick. This is the kind they used at the time of the Revolutionary War.

It just has a lot of old black powder.

Gunpowder! Be careful, it's still dangerous.

I think we found where they hid the ammunition!

Aunt Jane, the dirt in the woodshed looked as if it had been moved. There's a stranger around here.

A NEW DISCOVERY

We've been waiting for you. Can you tell us anything new about the flintlock gun?

I think I can.

The next day, Mr. Cole's brother arrived. He wanted to meet the Aldens, since he'd heard so much about them.

"You see, I knew Andy Bean had that flintlock. He showed it to me as a secret when we were boys. He had gunpowder and matches."

"But I suppose the gun was rusty. Before Andy knew it, he had started a big fire. Andy was afraid somebody would put him in jail, so he ran away."

Andy told me he found the gun somewhere in your house.

After that interesting story, the Aldens started to piece together the puzzle of where Andy found the gun.

Benny, where would you begin?

The potato pit.

The group quickly went down into the farm's potato pit.

Look over here!

Jessie and Henry removed the dirt from the wall.

There was a door, just like in the woodshed!

JUST IN TIME!

Behind the door was a secret compartment similar to the one in the woodshed. Inside were a milk stool, some dishes, and iron boxes that held gunpowder.

Grandfather helped them haul their new discoveries out to the yard to show Aunt Jane.

All these years we lived here, nobody ever found that door.

I'm sure someone hid from the Redcoats in those caves!

Oh, I'm tired out thinking!

All of this goes back to Andy Bean. He must have found the gun in the secret place in the cellar!

Andy Bean! All the trouble he's made running away and all. I never want to see him again!

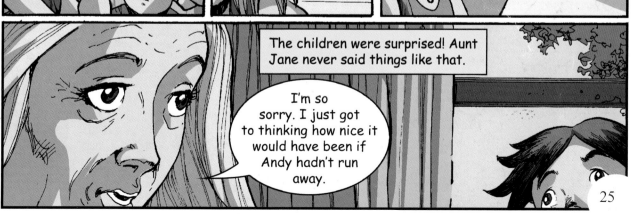

The children were surprised! Aunt Jane never said things like that.

I'm so sorry. I just got to thinking how nice it would have been if Andy hadn't run away.

25

The next day, the Aldens went back to the woodshed. Henry thought they may find something new.

Someone's coming.

Oh, hello! Do you live around here?

I used to. But it wasn't a good idea to come back.

She hates me! She never wants to see me again.

The children weren't sure who the man was talking about...

After the man left, the Aldens continued to the woodshed.

That man was strange! I wonder who he was...

When they arrived, they found it empty again.

We've explored all around here. There isn't anywhere else a person could stay.

I bet that man was staying here!

All his things are gone now.

Only Andy Bean knew about that hiding place. It must have been Andy staying here.

Let's go get Grandfather! We must catch Andy!

27

AUNT JANE'S SURPRISE

The Aldens rushed to the bus station. The bus was just leaving.

Thank you for stopping! We're looking for someone.

Are you Andy Bean?

Yes, I am.

28

The Aldens brought Andy back to the farm. There, Andy told them he had read in the paper that the Aldens had bought the old house.

He came up to see if he was welcome.

You were the one stealing all those eggs!

Well, the farm **does** belong to my family.

I have a long story to tell. But first I have something for you.

Everywhere I went, I bought you a jewel.

Why didn't you come home?

I was afraid. Then when you moved, I didn't have a reason to come back.

Andy had one more secret to share...

Andy shared a letter that told of the Coopers, who lived on the farm during the Revolutionary War.

They hid weapons, ammunition, and sometimes people in the woodshed and potato pit. They hoped to help make this country free.

"Long ago, I found something exciting. I tried to get Jane to go look at it, but she wouldn't."

I suppose the Coopers acted strangely and many people would make up stories about this place.

We'll have the real story to tell now.

Another mystery solved!

Even though Andy and Jane were no longer young, they knew that they were meant for each other. Soon they married, and everyone celebrated.

ABOUT THE CREATOR

Gertrude Chandler Warner was born on April 16, 1890, in Putnam, Connecticut. In 1918, Warner began teaching at Israel Putnam School. As a teacher, she discovered that many readers who liked an exciting story could not find books that were both easy and fun to read. She decided to try to meet this need. In 1942, *The Boxcar Children* was published for these readers.

Warner drew on her own experience to write *The Boxcar Children*. As a child she spent hours watching trains go by on the tracks near her family home. She often dreamed about what it would be like to live in a caboose or freight car—just as the Alden children do.

When readers asked for more Alden adventures, Warner began additional stories. While the mystery element is central to each of the books, she never thought of them as strictly juvenile mysteries. She liked to stress the Aldens' independence. Henry, Jessie, Violet, and Benny go about most of their adventures with as little adult supervision as possible—something that delights young readers.

During her lifetime, Warner received hundreds of letters from fans as she continued the Aldens' adventures, writing nineteen Boxcar Children books in all. After her death in 1979, her publisher, Albert Whitman and Company, carried on Warner's vision. Today, the Boxcar Children series has more than 100 books.